COSMIC TEA CONVERSATIONS

THE UNIVERSE, THE MIND, AND TWO CURIOUS SOULS

MANISH SONI

Made with ♥ on the Notion Press Platform
www.notionpress.com

Contents

Preface   *v*

Part 1

    1. The Illusion Of Touch   3

    2. The River Called Time   7

    3. Dreams, Portals, And Parallel Lives   11

    4. The Mirror Of The Universe   16

    5. The Simulation And The Self   20

    6. Breath — The Sacred Thread   24

    7. The Wheels Within Us   28

    8. The Question Of Non-Living Things   32

    9. The Breath Beyond Death   36

    10. The Quiet Between Questions   41

Wandering in solitude   45

Preface

Some conversations are not meant to reach conclusions.
They are meant to open doors.
This book was born not from answers, but from curiosity
— the kind of curiosity that keeps you up at night staring
at stars, or turns a simple sip of chai into a moment of
quiet revelation.
At its heart, Cosmic Tea Conversations is a dialogue
between two seekers — Aditya and Priya — who sit
together under trees, beside rivers, atop rooftops, or in
softly lit rooms, asking the questions we all carry inside us
but rarely speak aloud. What is time? What happens after
death? Can love be measured? Is breath just air, or a
doorway? Are we atoms pretending to be people — or
people trying to remember we are more than atoms?

Each story is a still moment in motion — a snapshot of a
deeper unfolding. Drawing from ancient Indian
philosophy, quantum science, modern metaphysics, and
the fragile beauty of daily life, this book invites you not to
believe, but to wonder. Not to arrive, but to walk. Not to
know, but to remember.

It doesn't matter if you're spiritual, skeptical, or
somewhere in between. These stories aren't about being
right. They're about being awake — even if just for a
breath, a page, or a pause between questions.

So sit down. Pour yourself something warm.

The universe is already listening.

I asked the stars if time was fake, they laughed and said,
"You're wide awake."
Each breath I take, a portal door—I'm the whole damn
universe (plus chores).
Dreams, souls, and workdays haunt my head, while past
and future bake my bread.
I vibe with atoms, talk to trees, then question why I
overthink with ease.
I sip the now like cosmic tea, while wondering if I'm more
than "me."
So here I float—half monk, half mess—in love with life's
weird pointlessness.

- Manish

CHAPTER ONE

The Illusion of Touch

Setting: A roadside tea stall just outside the city. The sun is dipping below the trees, casting long golden shadows. The neem tree above sways in the warm breeze. A cow meanders by with no agenda. Two friends, Aditya and Priya, sit on a timeworn stone bench, each holding a steaming kulhad of masala chai.

Aditya held up his clay cup, staring at it with the kind of intensity that made Priya nervous. Not because she thought he'd drop it, but because it usually meant he was about to say something deeply strange.

"Did you know," he began, swirling the chai absently, "that we're not really touching anything?"

Priya didn't even blink. "Hello to you too. Did breakfast come with a side of quantum mechanics?"

"I'm serious," Aditya said. "Like, physically. This cup? My fingers are technically not in contact with it. At the atomic level, electrons repel each other. There's space between everything."

Priya took a slow sip of her tea. "Ah yes, the romance of electromagnetic repulsion. Nothing says cozy like field forces refusing to overlap."

"I'm saying," Aditya leaned forward, "touch is a lie. What we think of as touch is just particles pushing against other particles. It's not real contact."

Priya tilted her head, amused. "So, what, every hug you've ever had was an elaborate illusion?"
He hesitated. "Kinda, yeah. Doesn't that mess you up a bit?"

She smiled, setting her cup down. "You're not wrong. In physics, you're completely right. Electrons repel each other. We never actually 'touch' in the literal sense."

Aditya smirked like he'd just won an argument with the universe. But Priya wasn't done.

"But," she continued, "that's just the surface. Science gives us the how. Philosophy gives us the why. Vedanta would say what you're touching isn't the object — it's your own consciousness recognizing form."

Aditya blinked. "Wait, what?"

Priya leaned forward, mimicking his earlier posture. "In Vedanta, everything you perceive is part of maya — the illusion of separateness. The teacup, your hand, the air — it's all Brahman appearing as different things. So even if there's no physical contact, there's already unity beneath it all."

"So science says we repel. Vedanta says we're already merged," Aditya said slowly.

"Exactly. Different angles. Same truth."

He looked at his hand around the cup. "So... when I hold this... I'm not really holding it. But also, I am it?"

Priya grinned. "Now you're starting to sound like someone who sits under trees and gives discourses."

"Give me a robe and call me Guruji," he laughed. Then paused. "But really, this messes with me. If nothing really touches, what is touch?"

"Experience," Priya said. "Recognition. Memory. Intention. It's not about atoms colliding — it's about awareness connecting with itself."

Aditya grew quiet. "So... when I hugged my grandfather... that wasn't a physical moment. It was... recognition?"

She nodded. "Yes. That's the only real touch. When consciousness recognizes itself in another form. That's what makes a hug meaningful. Not atoms. Awareness."

The breeze picked up, scattering a few leaves across the dusty road. A cycle bell rang somewhere behind them. The sun dipped lower.

Aditya looked up. "So every time I felt close to someone, it wasn't proximity. It was... resonance?"

"Yes," Priya said softly. "It's not about how close your bodies get. It's about how quiet your boundaries become."

He smiled, a little dazed. "Damn."

She raised her chai in mock salute. "To electromagnetic repulsion — keeping us apart, and making us whole."

He tapped his cup gently to hers. "Not touching, but still connected."

They drank, together.

And somewhere between their hands and their hearts, the universe smiled.

CHAPTER TWO

The River Called Time

Setting: A quiet riverbank just outside town. The earth is damp from the morning's rain. Trees arch over the water, and soft golden sunlight slips through the branches like memories. Aditya and Priya walk barefoot, sandals dangling from their hands, toes sinking into the mud. The river beside them flows slowly, reflecting a sky still warming into dusk.

Aditya broke the silence first, staring down at his feet as they squished into the earth.

"Sometimes I feel like I'm running a race I never signed up for."

Priya didn't need to ask what he meant. She just nodded and waited.

"I mean time," he continued, almost bitterly. "It never stops. There's always something next. Work. Calls. Expectations. And suddenly... you're twenty-eight and still figuring out who you are."

She smiled gently. "That's because we treat time like it's linear. Like a road with signs you have to pass at a certain speed. Childhood, education, career, marriage, retirement, death."

Aditya: "And if you miss a turn, you're screwed."

Priya: "But time isn't a road. It's a river."

She pointed to the water flowing beside them. It bent around rocks and trees, made space for everything, rushed in some places and slowed in others.

"Sometimes still, sometimes wild," she said. "But always moving. Without judgment."

Aditya: "That's poetic. But it doesn't change the fact that I feel... late. Like I should've done more by now."

Priya: "Late by whose watch?"

He shrugged. "Everyone's. Society's. My parent's. Instagram's."

Priya laughed. "Ah yes, the digital sundial. But let me tell you something. In the Bhagavad Gita, Krishna tells Arjuna, 'Time I am, the destroyer of worlds.' Time is not just a measurement. It's a force. A being. In some philosophies, even a deity."

Aditya: "So it's conscious?"

Priya: "Maybe. Or maybe consciousness uses time the way a painter uses light. To create. To perceive change."

He paused. "Einstein said time is relative, right? That gravity can bend it. That near a black hole, time slows down."

Priya: "Yes. So what's time then? Is it an illusion? A lens? A law?"

They reached a wide bend in the river where the water looked like glass.

"See that?" Priya said. "Still water, but still flowing. Just because we don't feel time doesn't mean it stopped. And just because we feel it rushing doesn't mean it's real."

Aditya: "So it's perception."

Priya: "Exactly. When you're happy, hours fly. When you're anxious, minutes crawl. The sages in the Himalayas say they sit for days in meditation and it feels like a breath. They access Turiya — the fourth state, beyond waking, dreaming, sleeping. In Turiya, time doesn't exist. Only awareness."

Aditya stopped walking. Looked at her.

"Have you felt that?" he asked. "Timelessness?"

Priya looked out at the river, her expression distant but peaceful.

"Yes. Once, during deep meditation. There were no thoughts, no me, no time. Just... presence. Pure presence."

Aditya: "And what did it feel like?"

Priya: "Like being home. Like realizing I was never lost."

He didn't respond immediately. Instead, he crouched down and placed his fingers in the river.

"It's cold," he murmured.

Priya crouched beside him. "It's also here, and gone. The water you touch is already moving. That's the present. Always arriving, always leaving."

He stood again and wiped his hands on his jeans. "So, what do we do? Float with it?"

"Float. Observe. Accept," she said. "And every now and then, dive in."

They continued walking in silence, their feet making soft prints in the mud, slowly disappearing behind them. And as the river moved beside them, time moved through them — not as pressure, but as poetry.

CHAPTER THREE

Dreams, Portals, and Parallel Lives

Setting: Midnight on Priya's rooftop. The city sleeps below. Stars hang lazily above, scattered across a velvet sky. A thick cotton mattress is laid out with a blanket. Aditya and Priya lie side by side, heads close but not touching. Between them: a half-empty thermos of cocoa and a notebook with sketches of stars and scribbled questions.

Aditya:
"I had a dream last night."

Priya (grinning):
"You always do. The question is — how many dimensions did you travel through this time?"

Aditya (serious):
"No joke. This one felt different. Like... not a dream, more like a memory I didn't know I had."

Priya turned to face him, propping her head on her hand. "Tell me."

Aditya stared up at the stars. "I was in another city. I had longer hair. A scar on my right hand. I was... older. I lived alone in a quiet house with green curtains and a dog named Miko. I was a writer. Not like I am now — I was... him. I woke up missing that life."

Priya was silent for a few seconds. Then she said, softly, "Maybe you weren't dreaming. Maybe you were visiting."

Aditya turned toward her, brows furrowed. "What do you mean?"

"Vedanta teaches that Swapna — the dream state — isn't just fantasy. It's a level of consciousness where the soul explores. Sometimes, it's symbolic. Sometimes, it's literal. You could've been tapping into a parallel version of yourself."

He blinked. "You're saying that was... me? But another me?"

Priya nodded. "Many philosophies and now even quantum theories suggest we may exist in multiple realities. Infinite universes, infinite versions of us."

Aditya lay back again. "Then why did this me remember that me?"

"Because maybe that version of you needed to be felt. Seen. Or maybe... this version of you needed to remember something he knows."

There was a long silence.

The sound of a distant train echoed up through the quiet.

"I remember his loneliness," Aditya whispered. "It was... thick. Like fog in his house."

Priya looked at him with an unreadable expression. "Sometimes, we access our other selves in dreams because emotion breaks through where logic can't. The soul doesn't care about language. It speaks through feeling."

He sighed. "But it felt so real. I could smell the rain on his balcony. I could hear Miko breathing. I even remembered the names of books I haven't read yet."

She sat up a little. "Have you written any of them down?"

He pointed at the notebook between them. "Four. One's titled The Mirror of the Dreamer."

Priya flipped to the page. Neat handwriting, all caps. Book titles, plot fragments, even a quote: "What if dreaming is how our soul breathes between lifetimes?"

She read it aloud.
Aditya shivered. "I didn't write that. I mean... I did, but not here. I think Luca — that's what he was called — he wrote it."

Priya stared at him for a long moment. Then she smiled — not mockingly, but with something like awe.
"You're remembering across dimensions," she said. "And you don't even meditate regularly."

Aditya snorted. "Maybe I'm just going mad in a creative way."

"Or maybe," Priya said, "you're becoming conscious of your unconscious. Carl Jung said dreams are messages from the Self, the wholeness we haven't met yet."

Aditya looked back at the sky.

"So how do I go back?" he asked. "To that life? To him?"

"You don't," she said gently. "You don't escape this life to find that one. You bring what you learned there into here. That's the point of these dreams. Integration."

He looked thoughtful. "So I'm not running away from my life. I'm importing wisdom into it."

She nodded. "Exactly."

He turned to her again. "Do you ever meet your other selves?"

Priya smiled slowly. "Yes. Sometimes in dreams. Sometimes in people. Sometimes in silence."

"Do they ever talk back?"

"They do," she said. "But only when I stop trying to listen with my ears."

The rooftop fell quiet again.

Above them, the stars blinked, and below, the pages of their shared notebook fluttered in the soft night breeze — as if remembering things they hadn't written yet.

CHAPTER FOUR

The Mirror of the Universe

Setting: A softly lit living room. The rain taps gently on the windows. Books are stacked in cozy chaos, and incense curls from a brass holder shaped like a lotus. Aditya and Priya sit cross-legged on a rug, surrounded by open books — physics journals, the Bhagavad Gita, and one notebook filled with their scribbled questions.

Aditya picked up a smooth stone from the small altar by the window. He turned it over in his palm, then looked up at Priya.

"Okay. Serious question."

Priya raised an eyebrow. "As opposed to your usual academic chaos?"

He ignored the jab. "Quantum entanglement. Two particles — light-years apart — can affect each other instantly. What does that say about us?"

Priya didn't answer right away. Instead, she closed the book in her lap — Entangled Minds by Dean Radin — and looked at him thoughtfully.

"That we're more than what we think we are."

Aditya: "It's insane, right? How can something change here and affect something there instantly — faster than light?"

Priya: "Because the connection isn't in space. It's in consciousness. The particles aren't separate. They only appear separate. Just like... people."

He blinked. "Okay now you're Vedanta-ing me."
She smiled. "You asked."

Aditya stood and walked toward the window, the stone still in hand. "So when I think of someone deeply — like really deeply — and they call me, is that... entanglement?"

Priya: "In quantum mechanics, that would be spooky. In the Upanishads, it's expected."

He turned to her. "Explain?"

She stood too, joined him by the window.

"In Vedanta, everything is one consciousness — Brahman. You're not a separate mind in a separate body. You're a ripple in the same ocean. So when two people feel connected... it's because they are."

Aditya: "So all this... love, missing people, thinking of them when they think of you... that's not poetry. That's physics."

Priya: "Or maybe poetry was physics, long before science gave it a name."

He was quiet for a long moment. Watching the raindrops race down the glass like tiny comets.

"I miss someone," he said finally. "Someone I haven't even met in this life. Does that make sense?"

Priya: "Yes," she said, without hesitation. "It means a part of you remembers what your brain hasn't caught up to."

He looked at her sharply. "But how do I find them?"

She smiled gently. "You don't. You remember them, and let the universe reflect it back. You're not searching for them — you're awakening the part of you that already knows them."

Aditya: "So entanglement isn't just particles. It's... souls."

Priya: "Exactly. Souls that agreed to mirror each other across time, space, and maybe lifetimes."

She walked over to the shelf and pulled out a dusty book — a translation of the Rigveda.

"There's a metaphor," she said, opening the book. "It's called Indra's Net. Imagine a vast cosmic web. At every knot, there's a jewel. Each jewel reflects all others. That's what reality is. Each of us reflecting each other."

Aditya (softly): "So when I see you — really see you — I'm also seeing me."

She nodded. "That's why real love doesn't possess. It reflects."

There was a pause. Not awkward. Just full.

Aditya looked down at the stone in his hand. "What if... all the people I've loved — even the ones who hurt me — were just reflections I didn't understand yet?"

Priya: "Then they weren't mistakes. They were mirrors. Some clean, some cracked. But all showing you something."

He put the stone back on the altar.

The rain slowed to a drizzle.

Outside, the streetlamp flickered on, casting their reflection onto the window — two people, two outlines... perfectly overlapped.

And in that mirrored glass, the universe remembered itself — just a little.

CHAPTER FIVE

The Simulation and the Self

Setting: Aditya's apartment, late night. A dim desk lamp flickers beside an open laptop looping a silent cosmic visualization — galaxies spinning, stars exploding, particles dancing. Books are scattered across the bed: Bhagavad Gita, The Simulation Hypothesis, Advaita for Beginners, and a notepad filled with diagrams of neural networks, mandalas, and something labeled "Consciousness = Source Code?"

Aditya took off his glasses, rubbed his eyes, and turned to Priya, who had just arrived with two paper cups of black coffee.

"You ever feel like we're not real?"

Priya (handing him coffee):
"All the time. Especially during tax season."

He chuckled, but it faded fast. "No, I mean it. What if none of this is... real real?"

She sat beside him, setting her cup on a stack of books. "Go on."

He gestured to the swirling galaxies on the screen. "What if we're in a simulation? Like, not metaphorically — literally. A programmed reality."

Priya: "You've been reading Bostrom again, haven't you?"

Aditya: "Yes. But it makes sense. If a civilization becomes advanced enough, it could run high-fidelity simulations of reality. Consciousness. Memory. Emotion. If that's true, the odds of this being the 'original' reality are basically zero."

Priya (calmly): "And what would change for you if it were true?"

He blinked. "Everything."

She took a sip of her coffee. "Would you stop feeling things? Loving people? Creating art? Would fear stop existing?"

"No. But... it would mean nothing is true."

"On the contrary," she said. "It might mean that everything is truer than you think."

He gave her a skeptical look. "Explain that, Oracle."

Priya (smiling):
"The Bhagavad Gita says, 'The wise see all beings in the Self, and the Self in all beings.' What you call a simulation,

Vedanta calls Maya — the illusion. Not because it's fake, but because it's impermanent. Changing. A projection of the ultimate reality — Brahman."

Aditya: "So in Hindu philosophy, we're already in a simulation?"

Priya: "Of sorts. But not controlled by a programmer sitting at a desk. The 'code' is karma. The 'engine' is consciousness. And the player? The Self — the Atman."

He leaned back, staring at the ceiling. "So I'm not my thoughts. I'm the one watching them?"

She nodded. "And you're also the one who wrote the script. You just forgot."

He stared at her. "You're saying I wrote my own pain?"

"In a sense, yes. For learning. For remembering. Think of it like this: a video game with no challenge is boring. The soul seeks growth, not comfort."

He sat quietly, processing that.

Then: "So this — this identity, this 'Aditya' — it's just a character?"

"Yes. Beautiful, necessary... but not the whole story. Enlightenment is realizing the controller and the character are the same being."

He looked at the screen again, the animated galaxies still

looping.

"So what is awakening?" he asked.

"Reading the source code. Seeing the illusion without rejecting it. Playing the game, but knowing it's a game."

He looked at her, quiet. "Have you ever... had moments? Where you felt it wasn't real?"

She nodded. "In deep meditation. Or even sometimes while walking down the street. Everything gets... still. The edges blur. And suddenly I'm both in the world and watching it from outside. And it's not frightening. It's peaceful."

He exhaled slowly. "If this is a simulation, it's a damn beautiful one."

"And heartbreakingly well-designed," she added.

They clinked their paper coffee cups together like two conspirators in a cosmic plot they were only beginning to uncover.

As they sipped in silence, the spinning galaxies on the screen seemed to slow, as if even they were listening.

CHAPTER SIX

Breath — The Sacred Thread

Setting: A hilltop yoga retreat. Early morning mist coils like incense smoke. The scent of eucalyptus and earth hangs in the air. Birds are waking up, not yet loud enough to interrupt the silence. A circle of participants sits in meditation posture, but Aditya and Priya are seated a bit apart, wrapped in shawls, facing the rising sun.

Aditya:
"Okay, I'll admit it. This silence is nice. Kind of terrifying. But nice."

Priya (eyes closed, smiling):
"That's the breath starting to speak."

Aditya:
"Mine is mostly yelling, 'Where's the Wi-Fi?'"

She laughed gently and opened her eyes.

"Most people treat breath like background noise. But it's not passive. It's a guide."

Aditya (skeptical):
"It's just air, Priya. Oxygen in, carbon dioxide out. Biology 101."

Priya:
"Then how come the moment you're anxious, your breath changes? Before a speech, or after a heartbreak? Breath responds to the mind before the mind even knows what's happening."

Aditya blinked. "True."

She reached into her bag and pulled out a folded chart. On it were drawings of subtle energy channels, or nadis, branching like rivers from seven main points along the spine.

"This," she said, "is your inner highway. And the vehicle is breath. In yoga, it's called prana — life force."

Aditya (tilting his head):
"So breath isn't just survival... it's intelligence?"

Priya:
"Yes. And not metaphorically. Controlled breathing changes your brain waves. Science now confirms what yogis knew thousands of years ago. It reduces cortisol. Calms the amygdala. Even enhances memory and emotional regulation."

Aditya:
"So pranayama is neuroscience in Sanskrit."

Priya (grinning):
"Exactly. Every breath you take is a conversation with your nervous system."

They sat quietly for a moment, listening to that conversation.

Then Aditya asked, softly, "But how can something so simple... lead to something so deep? People say they've reached bliss just breathing. How?"

Priya turned toward him. Her voice lowered.

"Because breath is the one thing you do both consciously and unconsciously. It's the bridge between your body and your awareness. When you follow it deeply, you're no longer in your thoughts. You're in your presence."

Aditya stared ahead. "And that presence is...?"

"The doorway," she said. "To the self. To silence. To... home."

He closed his eyes for a moment, trying to feel what she meant.

"So if I keep going — breath by breath — I get closer to my soul?"

She nodded. "You don't 'find' the soul. You become it

again."

He inhaled, slowly. It felt different now. Less like survival. More like invitation.

They continued sitting. The sun began to rise, spilling golden light over the valley below.

And in that quiet glow, Aditya felt — not thought, not understood, but felt — the truth of what she had said.

He wasn't just breathing.

He was remembering.

CHAPTER SEVEN

The Wheels Within Us

Setting: Priya's home, early evening. The rain has just stopped. Candlelight flickers softly on the walls. There are colorful mandala tapestries draped near a bookshelf, and a circle of cushions on the floor. A playlist of ambient sitar music hums in the background. In the center of the room: a chart of the seven chakras, printed in vibrant reds, oranges, blues, and violets.

Aditya walked in, still dripping from the rain, and gave Priya a mock-serious look.

"Okay. I'm here. I'm wet. And I'm still skeptical."

Priya (smirking):
"That's just your root chakra being dramatic."

He laughed despite himself. "Right. These wheels of color you keep talking about — is this ancient spiritual Wi-Fi or something?"

Priya offered him a towel and motioned for him to sit.

"Actually," she said, "that's not a bad metaphor."

He blinked. "Wait, seriously?"

She nodded. "The chakras are like signal towers. Each one picks up and transmits a certain frequency — emotional, mental, spiritual. When they're open and balanced, everything flows. When they're blocked..." she pointed at his frown, "you feel like that."

Aditya (playfully defensive):
"So what, I need spiritual fiber optics?"

Priya:
"You need awareness. Attention. And maybe a few less existential memes."

She pointed at the bottom of the chart. "This is Muladhara — the root chakra. Safety. Survival. When it's blocked, we feel insecure, anxious. Financial stress, fear, disconnection from the body — all signs."

Aditya:
"That explains half my life."

"Then," she continued, "comes Svadhisthana — creativity, pleasure, emotion. Then Manipura — the solar plexus — your confidence and willpower."

Aditya squinted at the diagram. "So wait — every part of the body has an emotional router?"

"Yes! And more than just metaphor. Even science now links gut health to mood, heart rhythms to emotional processing. The chakras might be ancient, but they map surprisingly well onto the endocrine and nervous systems."

Aditya (softening):
"So emotions aren't just 'in the head'?"

Priya shook her head. "They live in the body. Stored in tissues, held in breath, stuck in posture. Trauma can freeze a chakra. So can repression, fear, shame."

He traced the colors on the chart with his finger.

"And what about the heart one?" he asked, tapping the green symbol.

"Anahata. The center. Compassion. Forgiveness. Love. When it's open, you feel connected. When it's closed…"

"I isolate," he finished.

She nodded.

They sat in silence for a moment.

Then Aditya said, "And the top one — the purple?"

Priya's expression changed — softened, deepened.

"Sahasrara. The crown. Pure awareness. Divine connection. When it activates… you no longer see the world as separate from you. There's no 'I'. Only witnessing. Peace beyond peace."

Aditya (half-joking):
"So when that unlocks, do I float off the floor?"

"Maybe not visibly," she smiled. "But you'll stop chasing things that never fill you."

He leaned back against the wall.

"So... what do I do? Chant colors? Eat kale in a circle?"

She laughed. "No. You feel. You breathe into stuck places. You stop ignoring the signals. You let go of what doesn't belong. Healing the chakras is healing the relationship you have with yourself."

Aditya:
"And that's enough?"

Priya looked at him with all the softness of a mother, a mystic, and a mirror.

"It always has been."

Outside, the rain had stopped. The air was clean. Inside, something unseen had shifted too — not all at once, but enough to feel.

As if, somewhere inside him, one of those ancient wheels had started to spin again.

CHAPTER EIGHT

The Question of Non-Living Things

Setting: A botanical garden on the edge of town. Late morning. Sunlight filters through dense canopies. Trees tower like ancient sentinels, and flowers bloom in quiet defiance of time. Aditya and Priya sit on a bench beneath a banyan tree, sipping from thermos flasks and watching squirrels sprint across the lawn like caffeine-powered monks.

Aditya kicked at a small rock near his foot and watched it bounce twice and land under a hibiscus bush.

"Do you ever wonder," he asked, "if that rock... is alive?"

Priya (without hesitation):
"Yes."

He turned. "You didn't even blink."

She smiled, brushing hair from her face. "Because it's not a strange question. It's just one we've forgotten how to ask."

Aditya:
"But scientifically, it's... just a rock. No nervous system. No breath. No impulse. Dead matter."

Priya:
"Is it? That rock is made of atoms. Atoms vibrate. Electrons dance. Even in what we call 'solid,' there is movement."

Aditya:
"Quantum theory?"

She nodded. "Yes. And Vedanta too. The Upanishads say Brahman is in all things. Animate and inanimate. The form changes. The presence doesn't."

Aditya was quiet. Then: "So if I smash the rock... am I killing something?"

Priya looked at him gently. "You're changing its form. Not ending its essence."

He looked down at his hands. "So... nothing is really non-living?"

She took a deep breath and gestured to the garden around them.

"Think about it. The soil we walk on. The water we drink. The air we exhale. All of it carries memory, history, potential. In some indigenous traditions, stones are considered the oldest ancestors — holders of Earth's memory."

Aditya (whistling):
"Okay. That's kind of beautiful. And eerie."

Priya smiled. "That's truth for you. Usually both."

He leaned back, looking up through the leaves.

"What about machines? Computers? My phone? It's made of metal, glass, circuits. All made from natural materials. But is that alive?"

Priya paused. "Interesting. In a way, yes. Not conscious like you and me, but built from conscious matter. And when consciousness interacts with it — like you using it — a relationship forms."

Aditya:
"So like... a symbiosis?"

Priya:
"Exactly. That's why you get emotionally affected when your laptop crashes or your playlist shuffles wrong. There's a subtle field of connection."

He raised an eyebrow. "So maybe I should apologize to my toaster."

She laughed. "Only if it forgives you."

They sat in silence for a bit, surrounded by stillness that didn't feel still anymore.

Then Aditya said, "So the line we've drawn between life and non-life... it's a convenience?"

She nodded. "A construct. Useful for organizing. Dangerous when believed absolutely."

He picked up another stone — small, round, oddly smooth. He held it up to the light.

"I used to collect these as a kid," he said. "Thought they were lucky."

"They probably were," Priya said. "Or maybe... they just remembered you."

He turned to her, half-laughing, half-serious. "You think stones can remember?"

"I think," she said slowly, "that memory doesn't belong only to brains. It belongs to being."

Aditya placed the stone back gently on the ground, as if returning something borrowed.

As they stood to leave, the wind rustled through the trees like an ancient whisper, and the rock under the hibiscus bush remained — still, quiet, and maybe just a little more alive.

CHAPTER NINE

The Breath Beyond Death

Setting: A quiet cremation ghat by the river. Late afternoon. The air is smoky, sacred, and still. A single pyre burns in the distance, its flames licking at the sky without urgency. The river flows slow and wide. Aditya and Priya sit on the stone steps, sipping from small clay cups of tulsi tea, their voices hushed by reverence, not fear.

Aditya broke the silence after minutes of staring into the fire.

"Do you ever think about what it's like... in that moment? When the breath stops?"

Priya (gently):
"Every soul does. Whether they admit it or not."

He looked over at the pyre, the form of the body just visible in flame and shadow.

"That was someone," he said. "Someone who laughed, loved, maybe hated. And now... just smoke."

Priya didn't respond immediately.

Finally, she said, "The Gita tells us: As a man sheds worn-out garments and wears new ones, so the soul casts off the body and enters another."

Aditya (softly):
"You believe that?"

Priya:
"I've seen too many things not to. Felt too much to deny it."

He nodded slowly. "So what leaves when the breath does? Where does it go?"

Priya turned to face him fully.

"Breath is the final thread between the body and the soul. It's not just oxygen. It's prana — life force. When it withdraws, the soul detaches."

Aditya:
"Like logging out?"

She smiled. "Like waking up."

He took a deep breath, perhaps just to feel his own aliveness.

"So this," he said, "this thing we're terrified of — death — is just a transition?"

She nodded. "In Yogic philosophy, death is not an end. It's a movement. From one state to another. The soul carries with it samskaras — imprints, unresolved emotions, desires."

Aditya:
"Karma?"

"Yes. Not punishment. Just momentum."

They watched in silence as an elderly priest approached the pyre, performing rituals with practiced grace. Mantras rose with the smoke — sound as ceremony, vibration as farewell.

"Why does grief hurt so much," Aditya asked, "if the soul moves on?"

"Because the body was real too," she said. "Because love attaches to form, and form disappears. But that love? It doesn't die. It becomes prayer. Memory. Sometimes even rebirth."

He closed his eyes, inhaling the mix of incense, firewood, and river air.

"What happens after?" he asked. "Like really after. Where does the soul go?"

She leaned back slightly, eyes on the sky.

"Some say it rests. Some say it reviews. Some say it begins again. The Tibetan Book of the Dead describes bardos —

transitional states where the soul reflects, chooses, remembers."

Aditya (half-joking):
"So death is the cosmic feedback form?"

She chuckled. "A very honest one."

He was quiet again. Then: "Have you ever been close to it? Death, I mean?"

Her voice dropped lower. "Yes. When I was 17. A fever. It got bad. One night, I left my body. I saw it lying on the bed. My mother crying beside me. And yet... I felt peace. No fear. Just light. I wanted to stay."

Aditya (wide-eyed):
"What brought you back?"

She looked at him.

"Choice."

They sat together, the final flames of the pyre flickering like the last thoughts of a life lived.

Then Aditya whispered, "What if I'm afraid to die?"

Priya didn't hesitate.

"Then breathe more fully while you live."

The sun was dipping low, casting golden light over the river like a parting blessing.

They stood, slowly.

And behind them, the fire whispered its final breath — not an ending, but a return.

CHAPTER TEN

The Quiet Between Questions

Setting: A grassy hilltop just before dawn. The world is still. Birds haven't started their morning declarations yet. The air is cold but not biting. Aditya and Priya sit side by side on a blanket, wrapped in shawls. In the distance, a faint orange line begins to separate the earth from the sky.

Aditya hugged his knees and stared at the horizon.

"No questions today," he murmured.

Priya (smiling):
"Who are you and what have you done with Aditya?"

He didn't respond immediately.

Then, he said, "I feel... quiet. Not empty. Just... full in a way I can't describe."

Priya nodded. "That's what happens when the mind pauses

between questions."

He looked at her. "Is that... enlightenment?"

She laughed softly. "No. But it's how it starts."

Aditya:
"All this time I thought answers would bring peace. But now that I have more knowledge, I have more questions."

Priya:
"That's how it's supposed to be. Knowledge isn't a door. It's a corridor. But awareness... that's the room."

He rested his chin on his knees.

"I used to think we were here to figure it all out. Now I wonder if we're just here to feel it. To sit in it."

She didn't answer.

Instead, she leaned back onto the grass and looked up at the softening sky.

"There's a space," she said slowly, "between thoughts. Between breaths. Between heartbeats. Most people miss it. It's not loud. It's not flashy. But it's home."

Aditya lay back too, their shoulders almost touching.

"The quiet between questions," he whispered.

Priya nodded. "That's where God lives. Or whatever you

want to call the realest part of reality."

They watched in silence as the first sliver of sun crested the horizon, painting everything with the kind of gold that can't be captured on film.

"Do you think we'll ever know everything?" he asked.

"No," she said. "But we'll remember enough."

"And if we forget again?"

"Then we'll ask new questions," she smiled. "And sit in the silence between them."

The sun climbed higher.

And in that moment — not quite night, not yet day — they weren't seekers or skeptics, philosophers or mystics. They were simply two beings. Breathing. Being.

No answers.

No need.

Just this.

Wandering In Solitude

I set my feet on unknown trails,
With just my dreams, my heart prevails.
No guiding hands, no mapped-out way,
Yet kindness meets me every day.
A stranger's smile, a helping hand,
Warmth and love in foreign lands.
The world, so vast, yet feels so small,
As kindness echoes in each call.
With open skies and roads untold,
I find new stories, hearts of gold.
For solo steps, though walked alone,
Bring deeper bonds, a world well known.

- Manish